I, DOKO

the tale of a basket

Ed Young

Philomel Books • New York

Adapted from a folktale appearing in various forms in Nepal and in many other Asian countries, most often conveyed in the oral vernacular.

PATRICIA LEE GAUCH, EDITOR

Designed by Semadar Megged. Text set in 18-point Charlotte Sans Medium.
The art was rendered in gouache, pastel, and collage.

Library of Congress Cataloging-in-Publication Data
Young, Ed. I, Doko : the tale of a basket / Ed Young. p. cm. Summary: A Nepalese basket tells the story
of its use through three generations of a family. [1. Baskets—Fiction. 2. Family life—Nepal—Fiction. 3. Nepal—Fiction.]
I. Title. PZ7.Y855Iae 2004 [Fic]—dc22 2003021535

ISBN 0-399-23625-2
10 9 8 7 6 5 4 3 2 1
First Impression

What one wishes not upon oneself, one burdens not upon another.

—Kung Fu Tze, Sixth Century B.C.

My name is Doko. It means "basket" in Nepalese. My master, Yeh-yeh, picked me from among many baskets. That was many years ago, when he, his wife Nei-nei, and their baby were all young and strong.

I was safe enough for Nei-nei to carry her baby inside me in the field. Sometimes Yeh-yeh used me to carry heavier things.

In what seemed a blink of an eye, the baby grew into a boy. I was with him when he helped the family gather kindling wood for cooking. We were always together, in fact, to carry this and that.

I still remember the year that the rain didn't come. Crops failed. How brittle I became. Worst of all, an epidemic took Nei-nei's life. It was I who carried her to her grave. After that, the boy and my master and I were left alone.

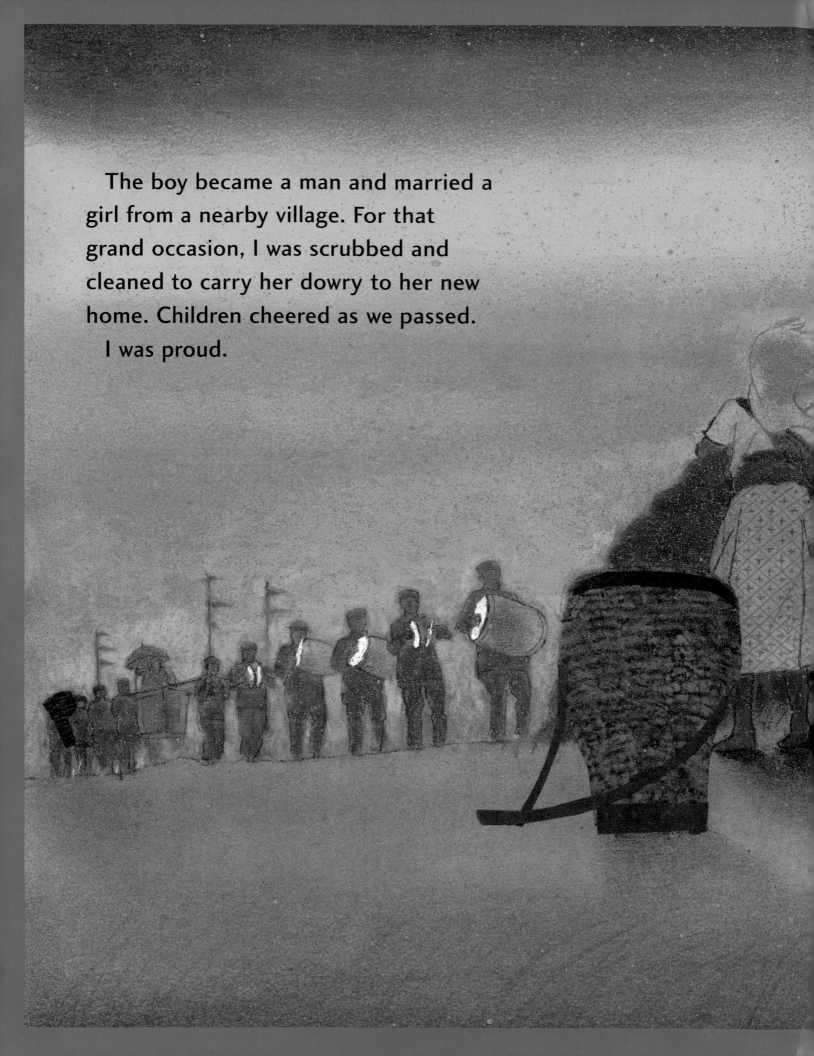

The boy became a man and married a
girl from a nearby village. For that
grand occasion, I was scrubbed and
cleaned to carry her dowry to her new
home. Children cheered as we passed.

I was proud.

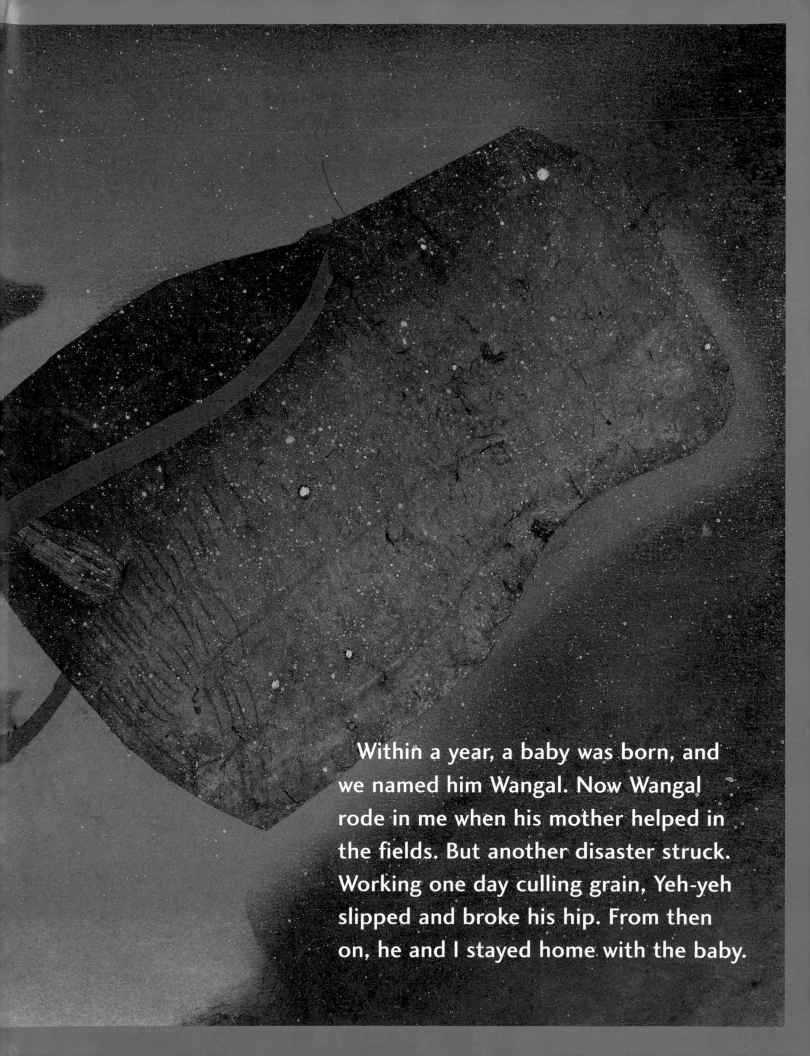

Within a year, a baby was born, and we named him Wangal. Now Wangal rode in me when his mother helped in the fields. But another disaster struck. Working one day culling grain, Yeh-yeh slipped and broke his hip. From then on, he and I stayed home with the baby.

Wangal, Yeh-yeh and I became inseparable as every
day we sat by the cooking fire and listened to Yeh-yeh's
wonderful stories.

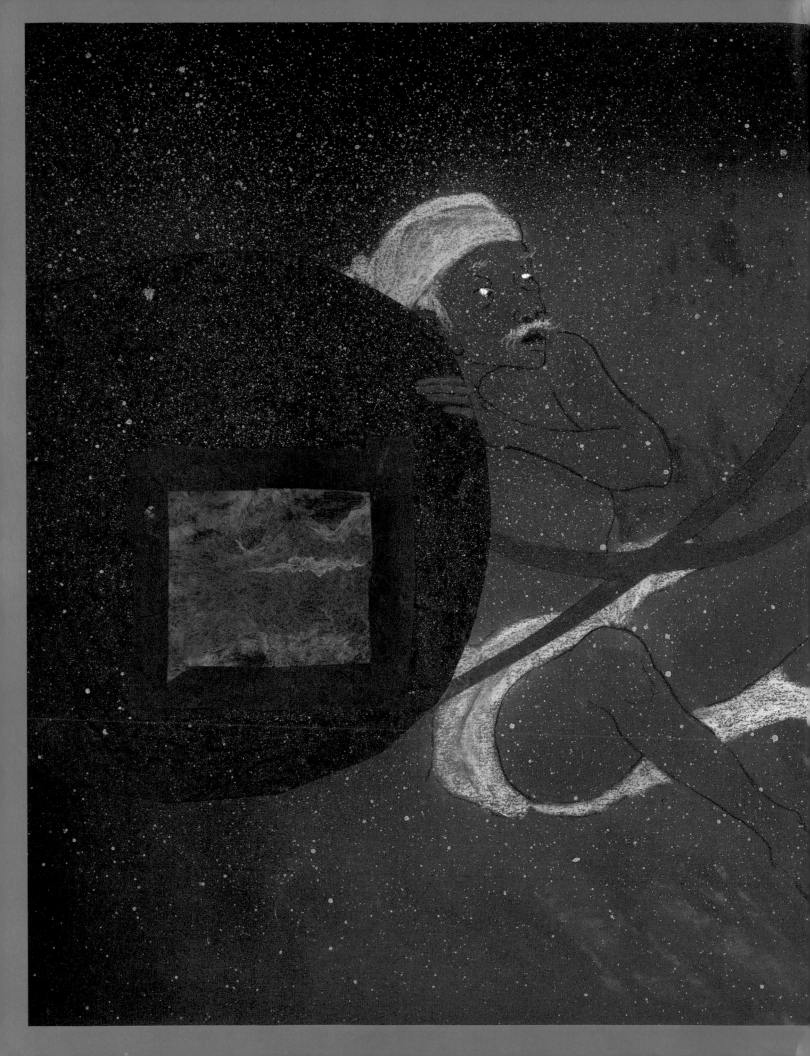

When Wangal turned ten, he, too, helped in the fields, leaving the aging Yeh-yeh home alone. I was often left, too. I was also growing old.

One day, a log rolled out of the fire near me and caused an alarm. Luckily, a neighbor stopped it from spreading. The man and the woman were nervous. How could Yeh-yeh have let the fire start! Now quarrels often broke out between Yeh-yeh and the young couple.

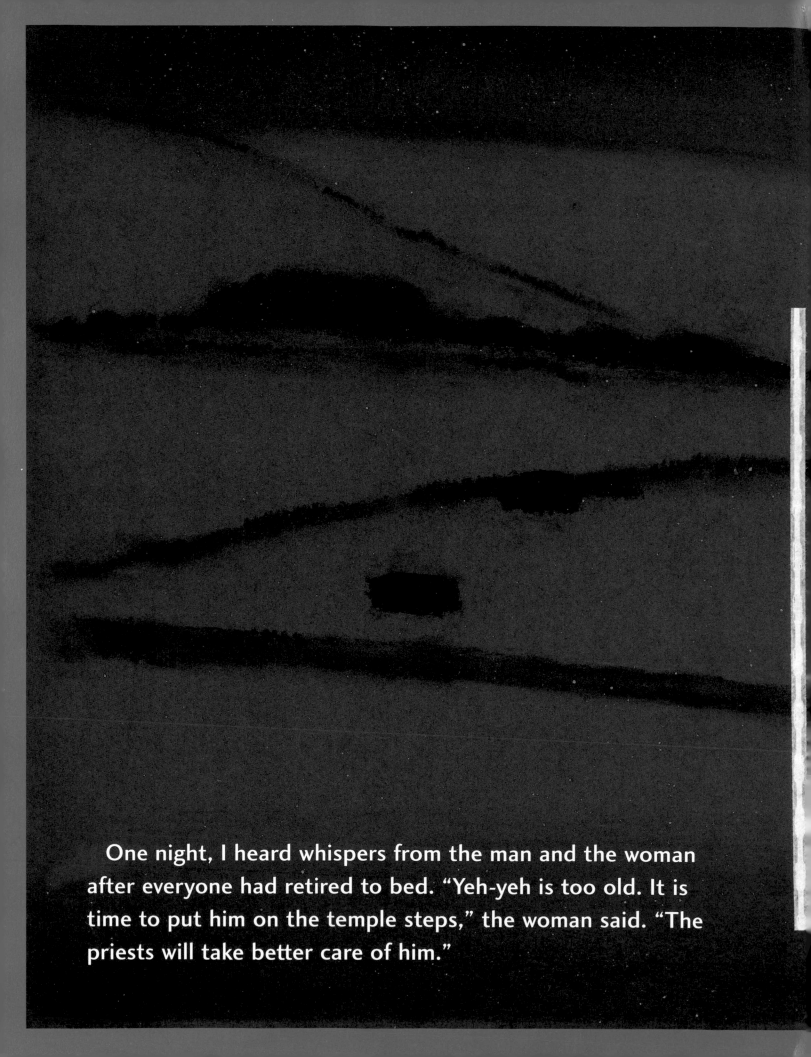

One night, I heard whispers from the man and the woman after everyone had retired to bed. "Yeh-yeh is too old. It is time to put him on the temple steps," the woman said. "The priests will take better care of him."

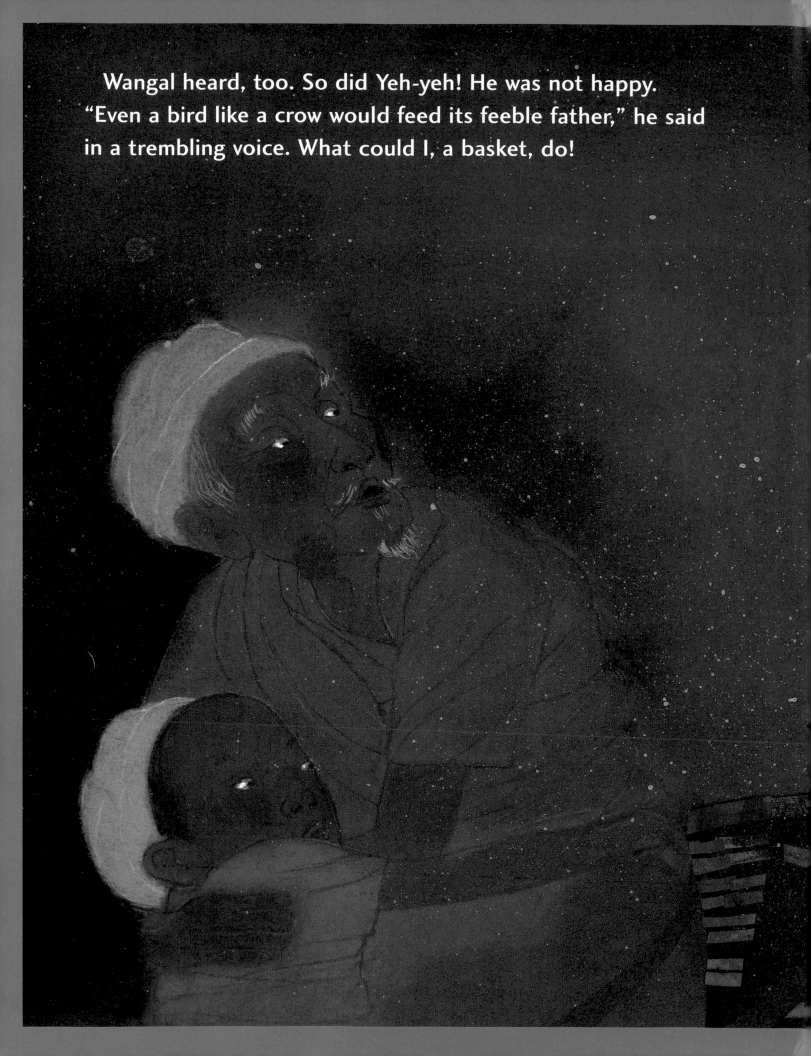

Wangal heard, too. So did Yeh-yeh! He was not happy.
"Even a bird like a crow would feed its feeble father," he said
in a trembling voice. What could I, a basket, do!

Early the next morning, before the mist
had risen, Wangal's father left the house
with Yeh-yeh inside me on his back.

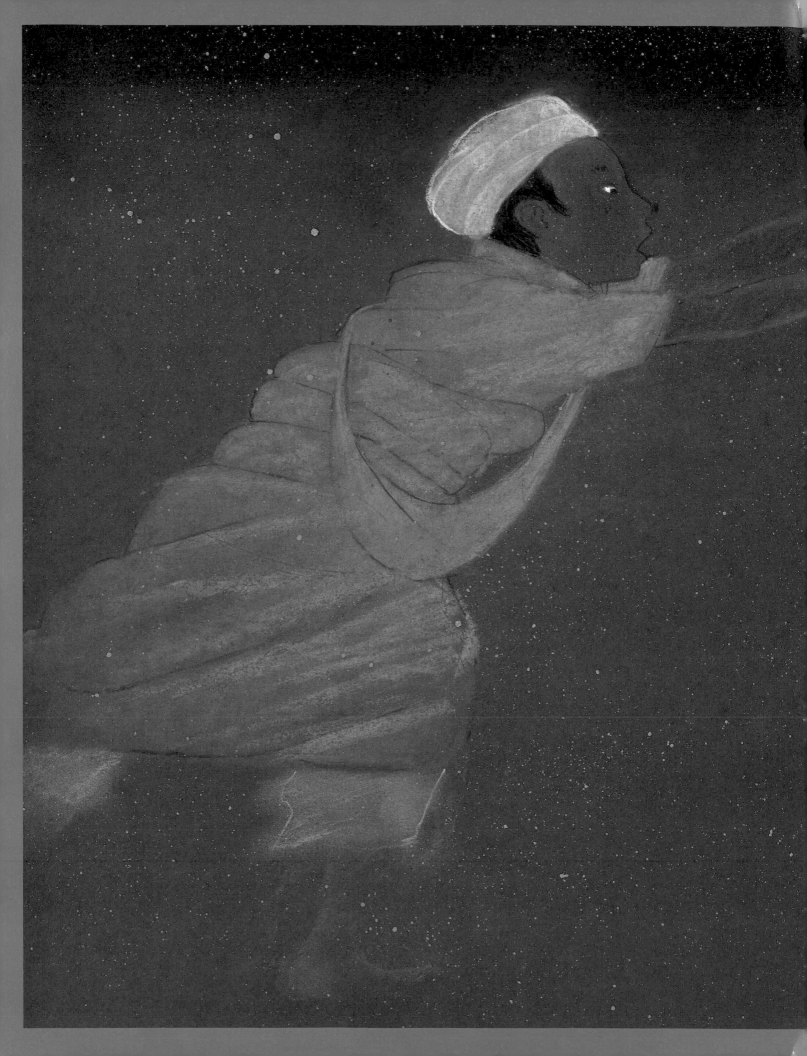

"Baba, Baba!" Wangal chased after us.
His father stopped. "What is it?"

"After you put Yeh-yeh on the steps, could you remember to bring Doko back?"

"What for?" grunted his father, glancing sideways at Wangal.

"This way," the boy said, "I won't need to buy another Doko when you are old and it is time to leave *you* on the temple steps."

At this, his father's mouth dropped open. He turned slowly back to the cottage without another word.

Wangal's love and respect for his grandfather inspired and transformed the whole village in how to treat elders, and from that time on, young and old lived out their lives in tolerance and harmony.